# Ant Storm

Anthony McGowan
Illustrated by Jon Stuart

# Previously . . .

In the story *Attack of the X-bots!*, the villain known as Dr X sends an army of X-bots to attack the children's new micro-den. He is after the children's special watches.

The micro-den is an old toy fort which is on an island in the pond in the park. The children set traps around it and manage to slow down the attack.

But there are too many X-bots. Things look desperate. Max is trapped. Then Cat has a clever idea.

She leads a group of ducks back to the island with a trail of bread. The ducks peck at the X-bots and fend off the attack. The children are safe ... for now.

# Chapter 1 – Ice-cream attack

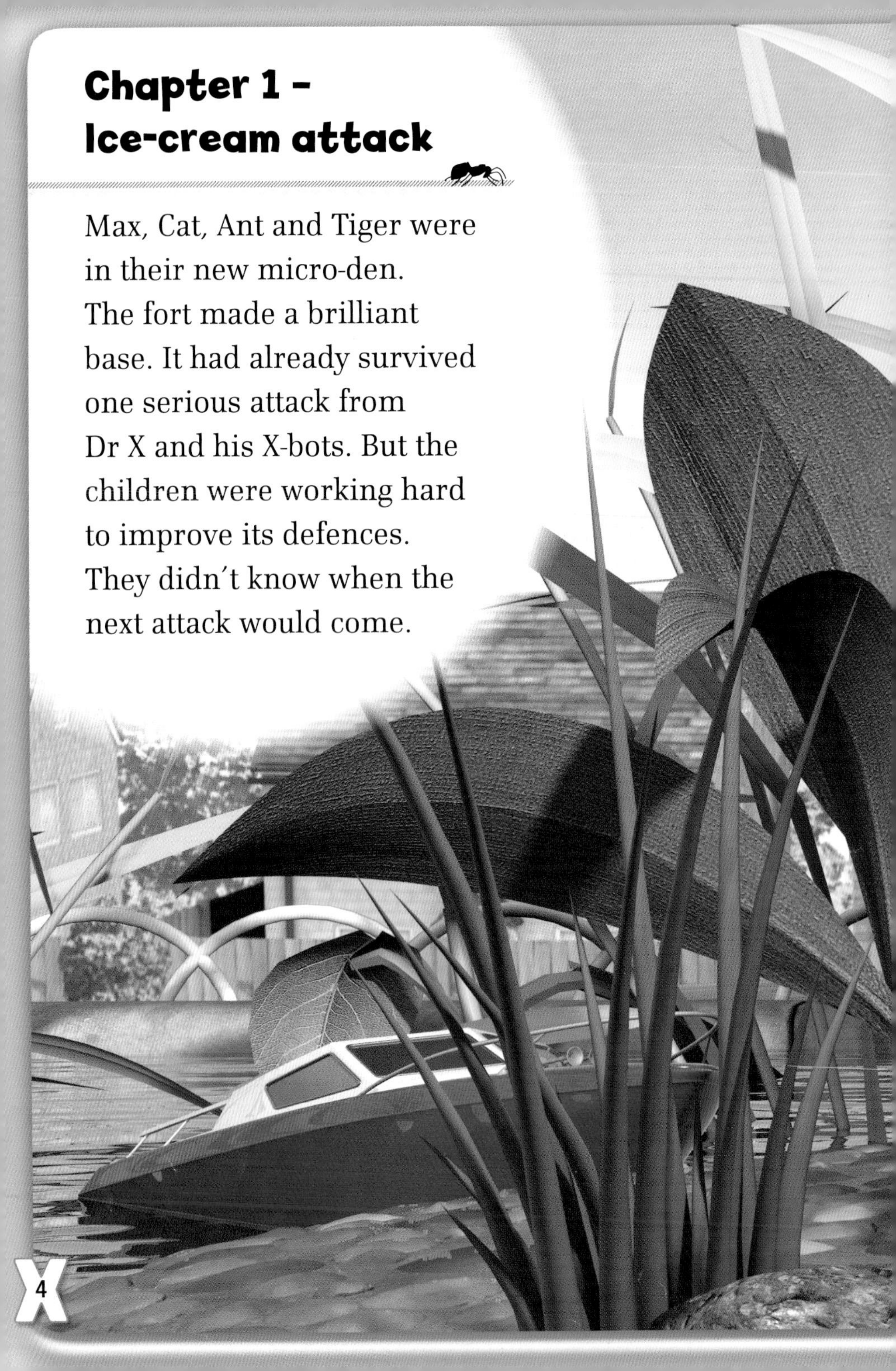

Max, Cat, Ant and Tiger were in their new micro-den. The fort made a brilliant base. It had already survived one serious attack from Dr X and his X-bots. But the children were working hard to improve its defences. They didn't know when the next attack would come.

They strengthened the walls by nailing up planks of wood – lolly sticks, of course.

They dug more traps outside the walls.

They even put in an early warning system - a network of cotton threads criss-crossing the little island. The children tied the threads to tin cans. Tiger's job was to put stones in the cans. If anything touched a thread, the tin cans would rattle and the children would know that someone - or something - was trying to sneak up on them.

Now they were having a rest. Max used his watch to grow back to full size and brought them all ice creams. Sadly, when he shrank back down to return to the island, the ice creams shrank as well!

They sat in the cool of the den and licked their ice creams.

Suddenly, Tiger yelled out, "Ant!"

"What?" Ant replied.

"Ant!" Tiger repeated. His eyes were bulging.

"What *is* it?" said Ant, getting a little annoyed.

"ANT!" was all that Tiger could say. "ANT! ANT! ANT!" He was pointing now. Max and Cat looked round.

"ANT!" they all yelled together.

Ant was cross. "Look, I'm getting sick of this –" But he stopped when he heard the scuffling noise behind him. He turned. The colour drained from his face. "ANT!" he gulped.

Before anyone could move, the ant lunged forwards, snapping its sharp jaws. Ant went cold. He knew that when an ant attacks, it never gives up. He closed his eyes, waiting for the end. But this ant was only interested in one thing.

*CHOMP!*

It grabbed Ant's ice cream and scuttled away.

# Chapter 2 – The sting in the tail

"Phew," said Tiger, "that was lucky!"

"That's easy for you to say," Ant replied, miserably. "It wasn't your ice cream! So much for our early warning system."

"It must have found a way through," said Cat.

"I'm a bit worried about this, guys," Max said. "Ant could have lost more than his ice cream. You're our animal expert, Ant – just how dangerous are those things?"

"Well, as you saw, they have a very strong bite."

"What do they eat ... apart from ice cream, I mean?" asked Cat.

"Mainly seeds and insects."

"Can they sting you?" asked Tiger warily.

"Some species can. But not the common black ant."

"So we should be OK then?" said Max.

"Well," carried on Ant, "they have got one nasty trick ..."

"Which is?" asked Cat.

"They can squirt formic acid at you."

"Oh, great," Tiger gulped.

"They use it for defence. As long as you don't bother them, they won't fry you with the acid."

"Well, anyway, it's gone," said Cat.

Max heard one of the cans outside the fort rattle. He looked over the top of the ramparts. "Don't be so sure about that," he said.

## Chapter 3 – Evicted!

The micro-friends looked over the wall. A head appeared in the bushes just outside the fort. Then another. And another. Soon dozens of ants were swarming towards the wall of the fort. There were too many of them this time to evade the cotton threads of the early warning system. The cans rattled noisily as the ants passed.

"We're being invaded!" gasped Cat.

"The first ant must have been a scout," explained Ant. "It must have taken the ice cream back to the others. Now, they probably all want one."

"Well," said Tiger, "they can't have mine." He quickly gobbled down what was left, smearing ice cream all over his face.

"Come on, guys," Max yelled, "we beat the X-bots, surely we can beat a few ants!"

He sprinted down the steps of the fort. The others followed closely behind.

"Who left the gate open?" puffed Cat, when they got to the bottom of the steps.

Ants were pouring towards the gate.

"Oh," said Max, "I think it was me ... when I went to get the ice cream," he explained. "Sorry, guys."

Cat shot him a look. "Come on," she said, and ran over to the pile of lolly sticks they had collected.

Together, they tried to force the line of ants back, using the lolly sticks. But it was no good. There were too many of them.

"We've got to get out of here," shouted Ant.

"Retreat!" screamed Max, forcing a path through the gates.

They ran out of the fort towards the safety of the bushes. There, they stopped to rest.

Ant turned to watch the stream of ants flowing towards the fort. There were hundreds of them now, approaching in a long line. They looked like an army on the march.

"Interesting," he said.

"That's not what I would call it!" said Tiger. "I'd call it a disaster."

Ant ignored Tiger. "The ants aren't interested in us at all. They just want to get inside the fort. Look ..." he said, pointing.

One ant was much bigger than the rest. It was leading a line of ants that were carrying squirming white grubs. Others held pale oval-shaped objects delicately in their jaws. They were being protected by very fierce-looking guards.

"What are they carrying," asked Cat?

"Those are the babies, called larvae, and the oval things are the eggs. That giant ant is the queen."

"What's going on?" asked Max. "Why would they want to bring the babies here?"

"It looks to me," Ant replied, thoughtfully, "as though they are moving the whole nest."

"What?" Tiger squealed. "They're moving it into *my* fort!"

The fort used to be Tiger's favourite toy before the micro-friends adapted it as their new base. He looked pleadingly at the others.

## Chapter 4 – On the trail

"Don't worry, Tiger," Max said. "We won't give up that easily. Why do you think they moved their nest, Ant?"

"Probably to avoid some danger."

"You mean they were attacked?" asked Cat.

"Could be, yes. Ants have lots of predators. Or their nest may have been flooded or something like that."

Max looked thoughtful for a moment. Then he said, "I think we should find out what's happened to their old nest and help them sort it out."

"We're going to help the ants?" gasped Tiger.

"If we can clear their old nest, they won't have any need for the fort."

"But how do we find the nest?" said Cat.

Max nodded towards the long line of ants, still filing towards the fort.

"Shouldn't be too hard, should it?"

The line of ants stretched on and on. Max, Cat, Ant and Tiger tracked back along the line. The ants ignored them.

"They're following a chemical trail laid down by the scout," said Ant. "Very clever, really."

Tiger shook his head. "Maybe you should go and join them if you think they're so great," he sneered. "They've already got a queen, so you can be king!"

Max interrupted him. “Ah, now I get it. I was wondering how they made it on to the island.”

The micro-friends were standing in front of a branch that hung down over the island. Some of the leaves reached right down to the ground. The ants were using it as a bridge.

“Come on then, guys, up we go,” said Max.

“You want me to climb up there?” shuddered Ant. “I hate heights!”

"Oh, come on," teased Tiger, "we've seen how good you ants are at climbing!"

"That's not funny," Ant snapped.

"Yeah, Tiger, be quiet," said Cat. "Don't worry, Ant, I'll go behind you."

The children made their way slowly up the branch. Max went first, followed by Tiger, Ant and then Cat. They were on their hands and knees, all except Tiger who was showing off by standing up.

“Get down, Tiger,” said Ant, “you might fall!”

“Just because you’re a scaredy-ant –” Tiger began.

He was cut off by a squawk and a fluttering of feathers in the branch above. A blackbird – startled by the noise – flapped out of the tree. Tiger looked up, stepped back ... and lost his balance.

Tiger felt himself falling backwards. He started to scream.

Then he felt a jolt in his arm as someone grabbed hold of him. He looked up. It was Ant.

Tiger looked sheepish. "Oops!"

"Well done, Ant," said Max, helping him pull Tiger back up.

"Thanks for saving me, Ant," said Tiger, when he was safe again. "And sorry I teased you."

"No problem," smiled Ant.

They carried on up the branch and over to the other side of the pond. There, the branch dropped down and ended near the bottom of the tree trunk. They climbed down until they were on the ground once again.

At the bottom of the tree trunk they found a hole. As they watched, the last of the ants came out and followed the others up the tree and across to the island.

"That hole must lead to the nest," said Ant.

"What are we waiting for then?" said Tiger.

It was Cat's turn to look worried. "It's very dark in there."

"Don't worry," Tiger replied, brightly. "I've got the light on my watch."

"And I've got my pocket torch," said Max.

So, with their lights shining the way, the children entered the dark hole at the base of the tree.

## Chapter 5 – Into the dark

Max had been hoping that they would find the ants' nest in the base of the tree but, when they got inside, all they found was a tunnel leading underground.

"Well, we've come this far," he said, glancing at his friends' nervous faces. "Let's see where it goes."

The tunnel was dark and dirty and Cat didn't like it at all.

"This is creepy," she said. "There could be anything down here."

"Nah," said Tiger. "Now the ants have gone, I doubt there's anything alive for miles around."

However, after a while, even Tiger began to sense that something wasn't quite right. Max and Ant felt it, too.

"Maybe we should go back," Ant said. "We don't know what we're going to find at the end of this tunnel."

"There's no way I'm giving up my fort to a bunch of ants," said Tiger, sticking out his jaw.

Max thought hard, weighing up the options.

"Let's give it another five minutes. If we don't find the nest by then, we'll go back."

"OK," said Cat, "just five minutes. But then we get out of this horrible hole."

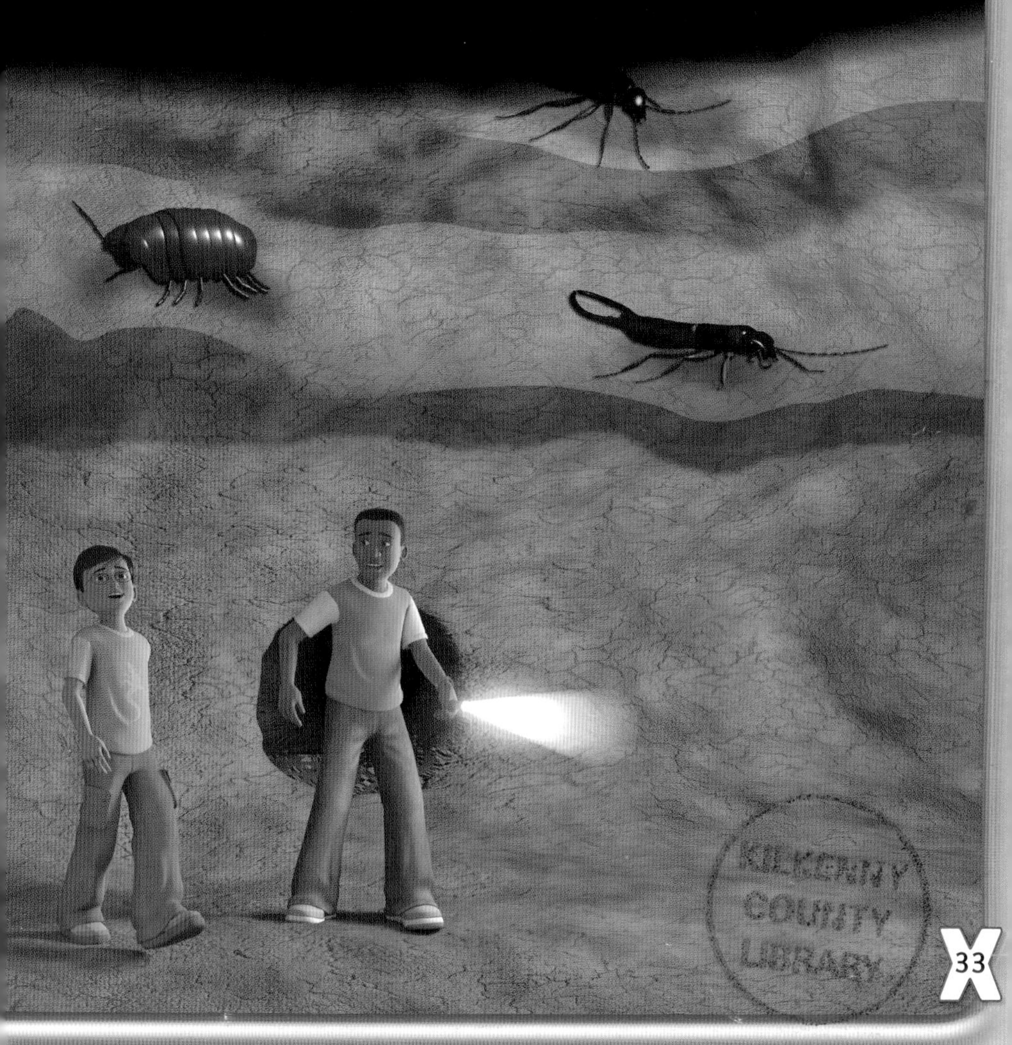

The air in the tunnel was hot and stuffy, and the walls seemed to close in around them. Cat tried to keep herself calm by whistling. The noise echoed off the tunnel walls.

After five minutes had almost passed, Max thought he heard something. He raised his hand and the others stopped.

"Ssshh, Cat," he said.

Cat stopped whistling and, as the echo died away, it was replaced with a soft scraping noise.

"What's that?" Tiger whispered.

"I'm not sure," said Ant quietly, "but –"

Before Ant could finish, a worm wriggled down from the roof of the tunnel behind them. A second later, a huge head burst through the roof after it, showering soil all over the children. The head had black fur, tiny eyes, a pink nose and sharp, gnashing teeth.

It was a mole, and it was on the hunt. It snapped up the worm, chewed it and swallowed. Then it sniffed the air hungrily.

"It takes more than one worm to fill up a mole!" said Ant, shakily.

"Run!" yelled Max.

They had no choice but to sprint forward along the tunnel.

"Is it chasing us?" Ant cried.

"I'm not waiting to find out," said Tiger, zooming past him.

# Chapter 6 – A worrying discovery

Eventually the children stopped running. There was no sign of the mole. They stood gasping for breath.

"Now what do we do?" Cat panted.

"I'm not going back," said Tiger. "Getting eaten by a mole is not my idea of a happy ending."

"We should go on until we reach the nest," said Ant. "There might be another way out."

"I agree," said Max. "But can anyone else hear a noise?"

"It's not the mole again is it?" said Cat, nervously.

"I don't think so. It's from up ahead somewhere."

They all listened. There was a faint sound of drumming.

"Sounds like thousands of feet marching," said Max. "Maybe not all the ants left the nest."

The children carried on, warily. There was an eerie light coming from the tunnel up ahead. As the children walked, the noise became steadily louder.

"Sounds more like baby elephants than ants," said Cat.

Finally, the tunnel came to an end.

Tiger looked down and saw the red X-bot alert was flashing on the screen of his watch.

Max saw it, too. He put his finger to his lips then switched his torch off.

The children crept forward, out of the tunnel and on to a ledge. They looked out over a vast underground chamber. It may once have been an ordinary ants' nest, but now it had been enlarged to a hundred times its original size. The children blinked as their eyes adjusted to the bright lights.

As their vision cleared, the children gasped in horror. The nest was full of X-bots. One side of the chamber was taken up with a big machine. The letters NASTI were painted on the side. A conveyer belt fed in various different-shaped pieces of metal. Fully assembled X-bots emerged at the other end.

As well as X1s, X2s and X3s, there were some new X-bots. They were twice the size of the others and had enormous pincers. They looked a bit like the ants the children had seen guarding the queen. But instead of guarding the queen, these X-bots were protecting the X-bot-making machine. They also seemed to be in charge of training the new X-bots which were marching up and down like soldiers on parade.

There were hundreds of them.

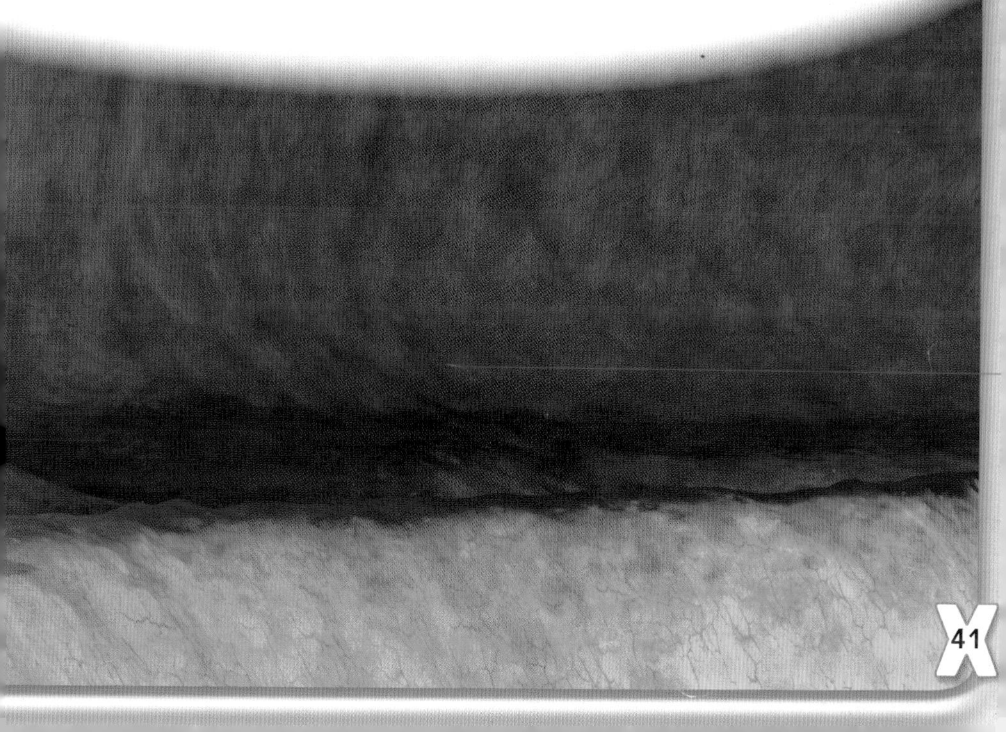

NASTI

# Chapter 7 – Not a happy ending

The children stared, open-mouthed.

"I guess we know now why the ants wanted to move house," whispered Max.

"This looks like some kind of mass production facility," said Ant.

"A what?" said Tiger.

"A factory."

"Yeah," said Max, "a very NASTI factory."

“I don’t like the look of those giant ant-bots,” said Cat. “Those jaws look like they could chop you in two.”

“You’re right,” said Max. “We should get out of here, then we can figure out what to do.” Max looked desperately around. “There’s another way out,” he said, pointing to a tunnel on the other side of the chamber. “If we creep around this ledge and jump down, we can get out of here!”

None of the children saw the shadow looming up behind them. It was Cat who heard the metallic sound first.

She turned ... and screamed.

One of the huge ant-bots towered over them. Its jaws opened up and, before the children could move, it spat out a net like a spider's web.

"Run for it!" yelled Max.

But it was too late. The net was already closing round them.

# Meanwhile . . .

Meanwhile, in his NASTI hideout, Dr X was sulking.

"It's my birthday and no one's remembered. Typical. Nobody cares about me around here. Not even a card. Perhaps I'll check in on the new X-bot production plant. That should cheer me up ..."

# Find out what happens next ...

Will Max, Cat, Ant and Tiger manage to escape the ant-bot's net? Will Dr X discover that they are there? Find out in *Ant Attack*.

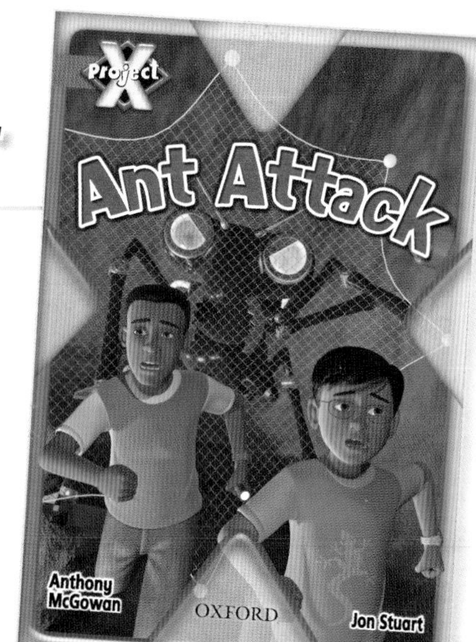